GEM

Emma Kallok

Illustrated by

Joel Bower

TRICYCLE PRESS
Berkeley / Toronto

TRICYCLE PRESS
P.O. Box 7123
Berkeley, California 94707
www.tenspeed.com

Design by Susan Van Horn
Typeset in CgGothic and Slanted

Library of Congress Cataloging-in-Publication Data

Kallok, Emma.
Gem / by Emma Kallok ; illustrated by Joel Bower. p. cm.
Summary: When a young girl's new sister arrives soon after her mother
hears a special song composed by their saxophone-playing neighbor,
the baby receives an appropriate name.
ISBN 1-58246-027-2 (hardcover)
[1. Babies--Fiction. 2. Racially mixed people--Fiction.
3. Saxophone--Fiction.] I. Bower, Joel, ill. II. Title.
PZ7.K1253 Ge 2001 [E]--dc21 00-010289

First Tricycle Press printing, 2001
Printed in Hong Kong
1 2 3 4 5 6 – 05 04 03 02 01

To my mom and my sister. —E.K.

To Mary Lou... You are always down the hall in classroom number three. —J.B.

The night is long, and I can't sleep. The silky moonlight slips around me like a *cool* sheet.

I hug my legs together and listen to *Bluesy Walker* play his saxophone to the stars in the sky...

...until my
eyes start
to close.

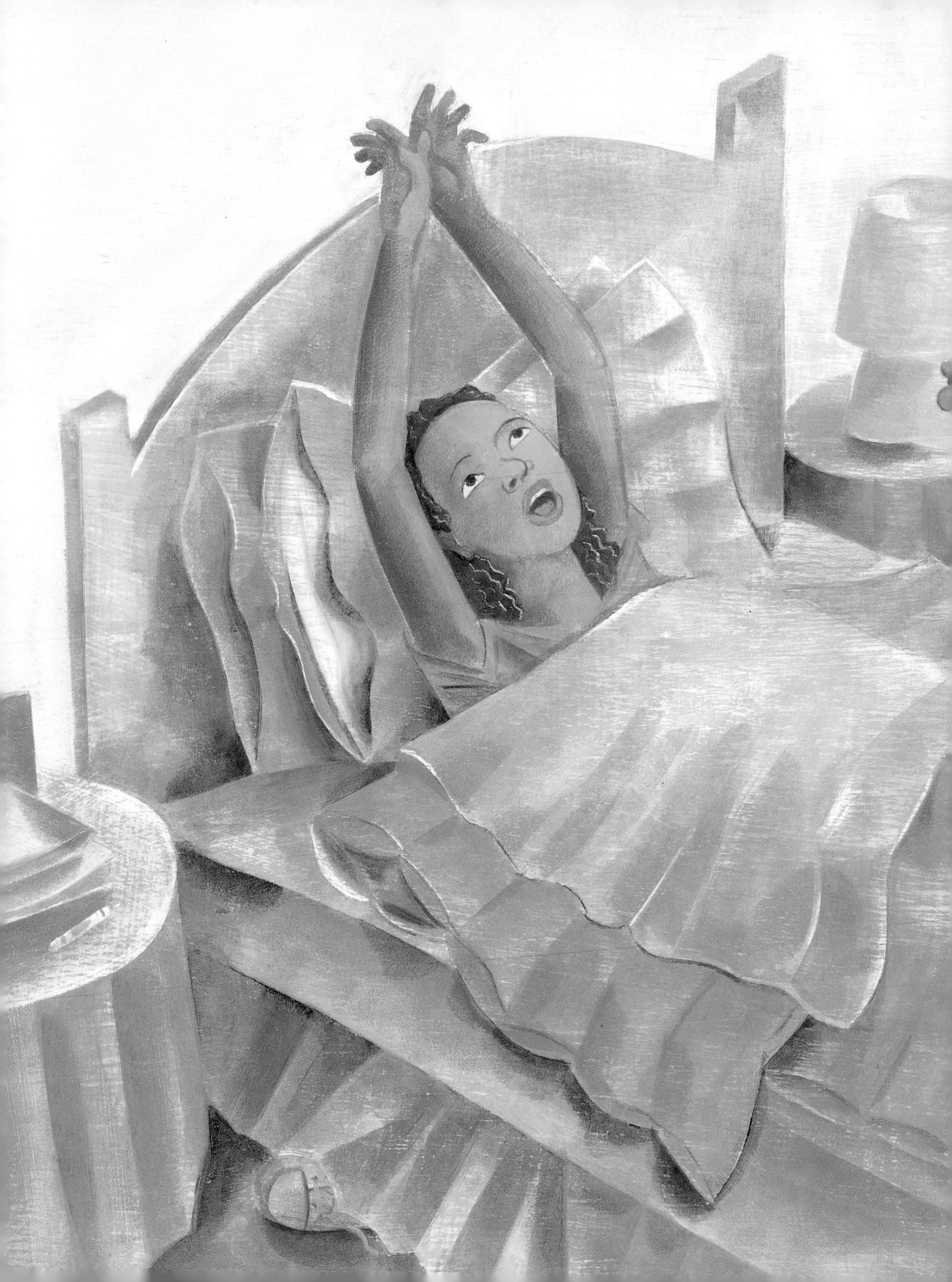

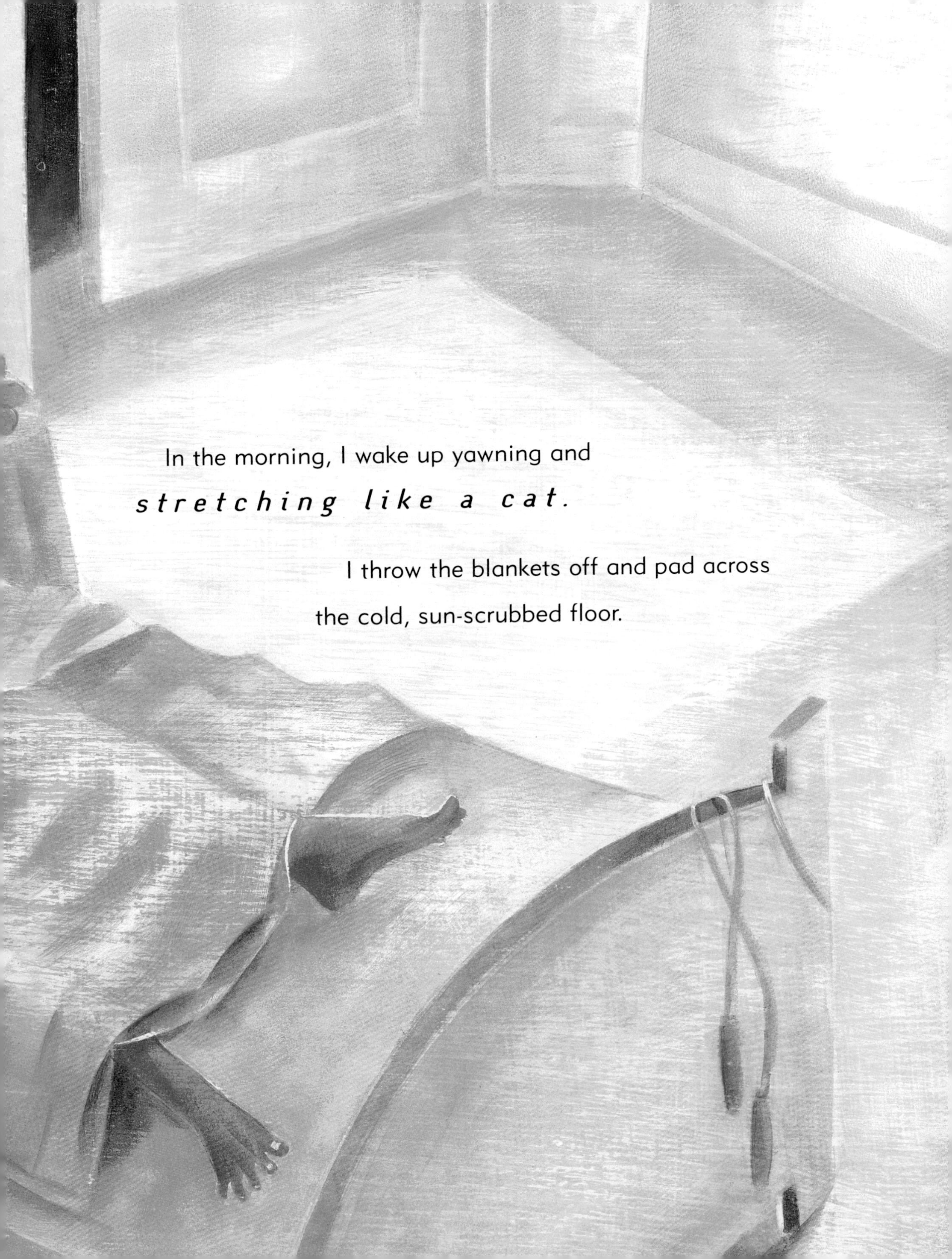

In the morning, I wake up yawning and

stretching like a cat.

I throw the blankets off and pad across

the cold, sun-scrubbed floor.

I find Ma in the living room smiling in her sleep. Her huge prize watermelon belly **bulges** from beneath her gown.

She looks happy.

Her hair *flows like honey* down the back of the rocking chair, where she has spent the night with her feet up. It's the only way she can sleep now.

I gaze out the window at the buds on the trees. I can't wait for my new baby sister or brother. The baby is due any day now. I am so impatient—like the Spring.

The house is quiet. Daddy's still out, working the night shift. I look at Ma 'til she wakes up. "Hi," I say.

"Hi," Ma says back. "Help me up, and we'll fix a special breakfast."

Bluesy Walker starts to blow his sax next door.

Bluesy is a good friend of our family's. He's a tall, tall black man. "The man with the sax," we say. Bluesy's gonna make his own record of the songs he plays, songs he calls *"gems."*

Ma and I make pancakes: lopsided golden disks with sweet strawberries, and **thick,** *oozy rivers* of maple syrup.

"Ask Bluesy if he wants to come play and eat something," Ma says.

I get dressed and *mosey* down the hall to Bluesy's, where I tap a rhythm on the door. The music halts and the door opens.

"Girlfriend! Put it there!"
Bluesy says, slapping me
high five, low five.

"Come on, Bluesy, come eat
and play those *gems*," I say.
"We got pancakes.
Big, special ones."

"Aw, you know
I love pancakes!
Bluesy Walker
comin' right up!"

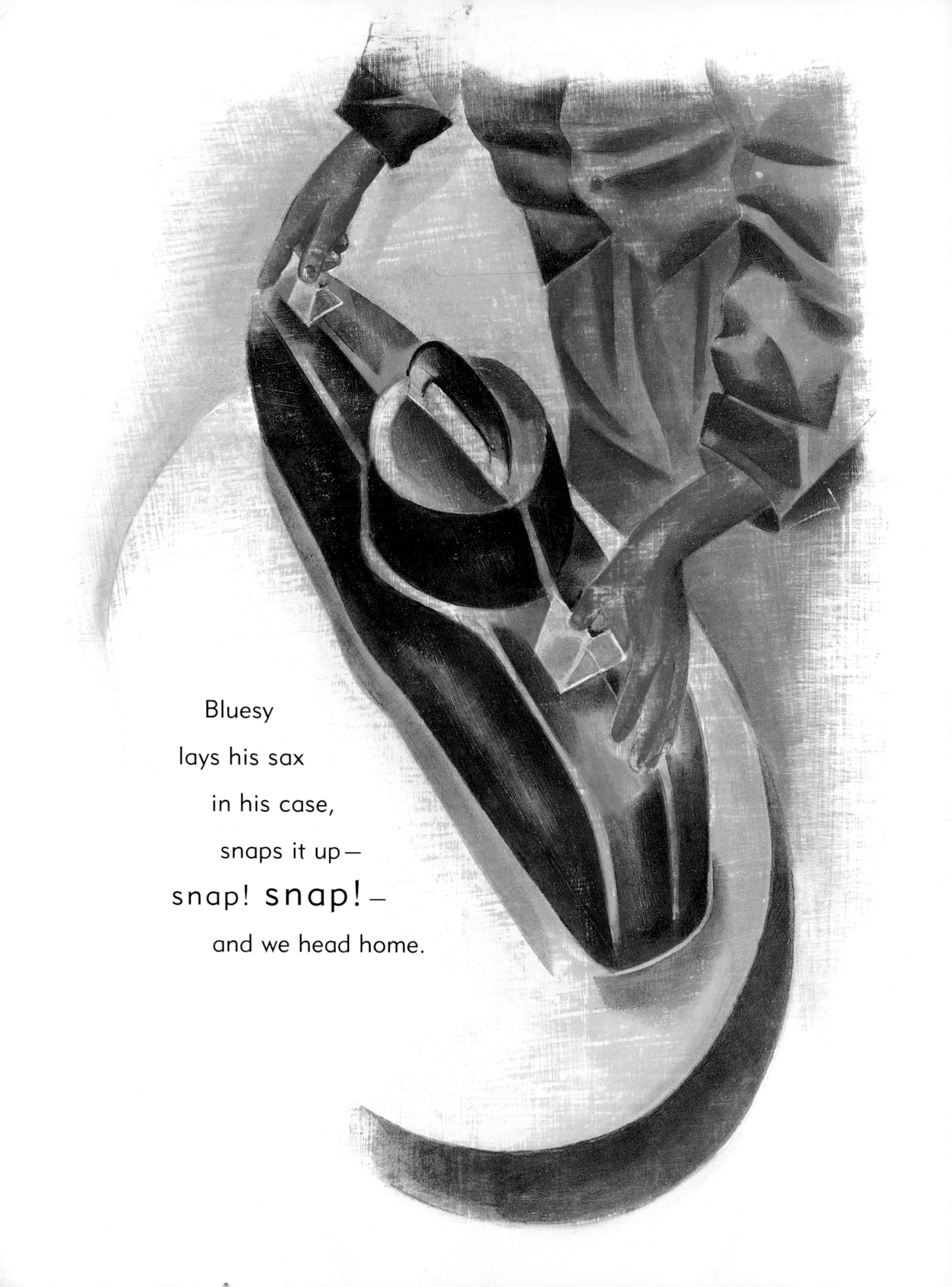

Bluesy
lays his sax
in his case,
snaps it up—
snap! **snap!**—
and we head home.

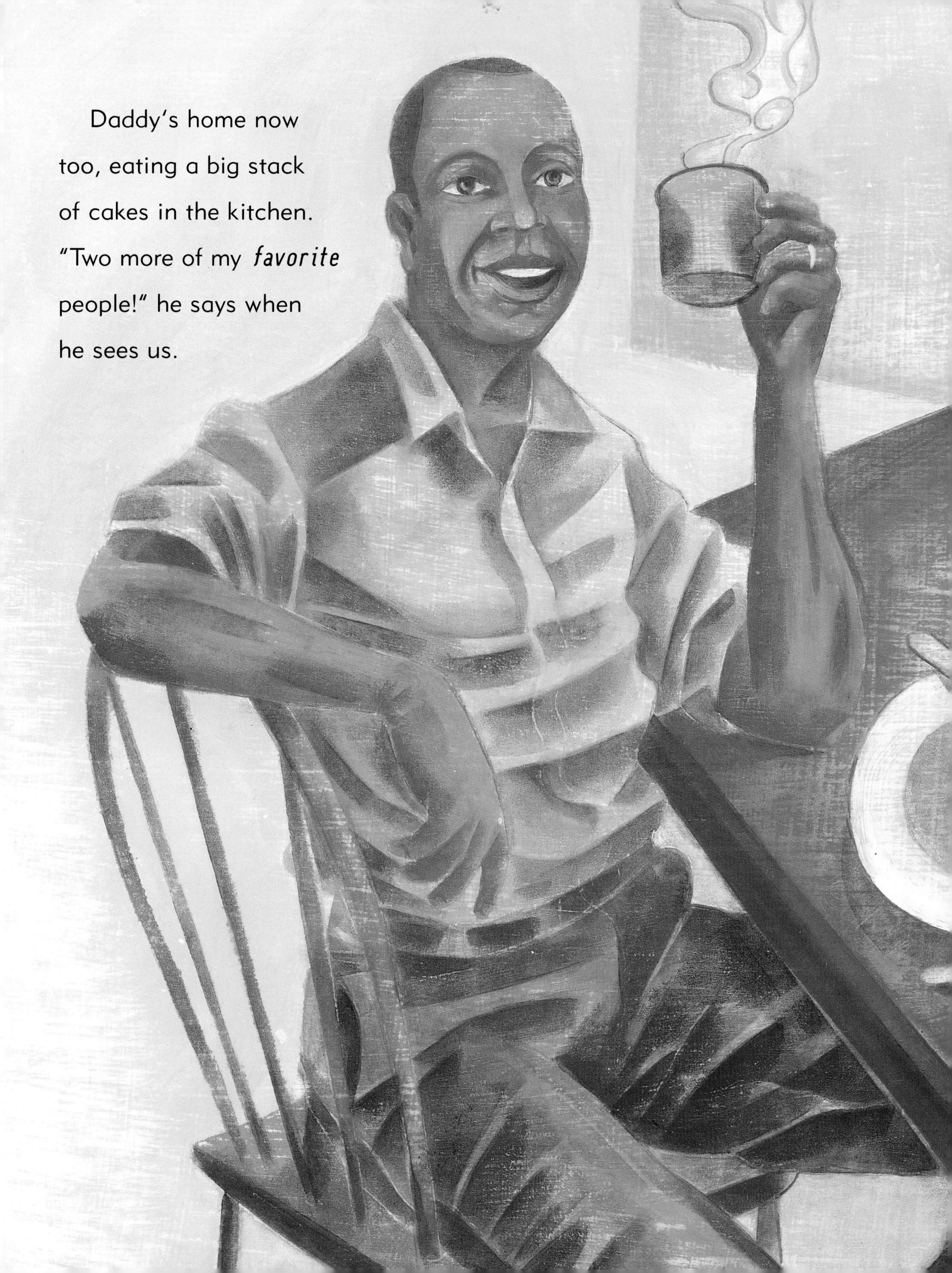

Daddy's home now too, eating a big stack of cakes in the kitchen. "Two more of my *favorite* people!" he says when he sees us.

Daddy gives me a big hug
and *whirls* me around.

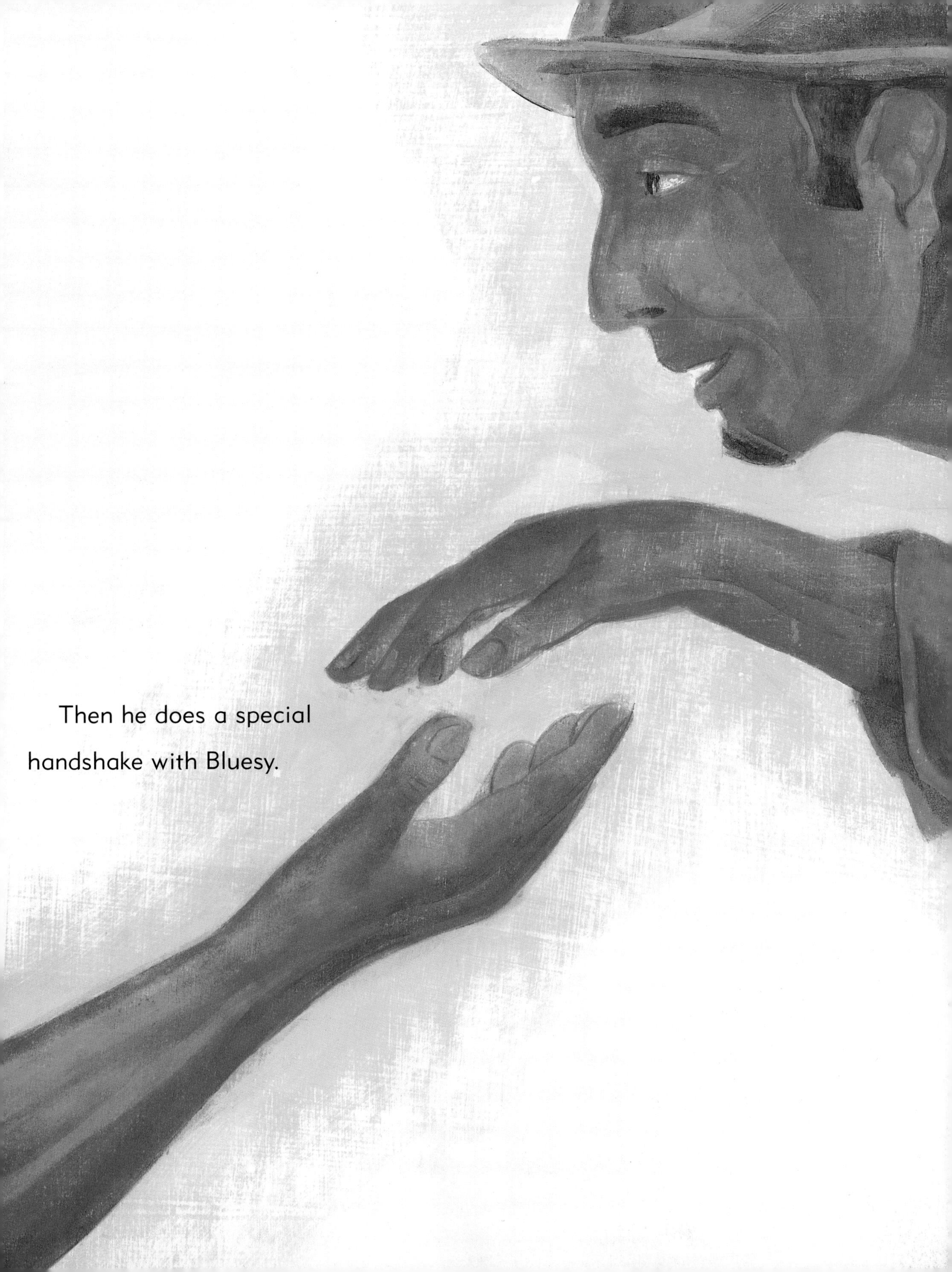

Then he does a special handshake with Bluesy.

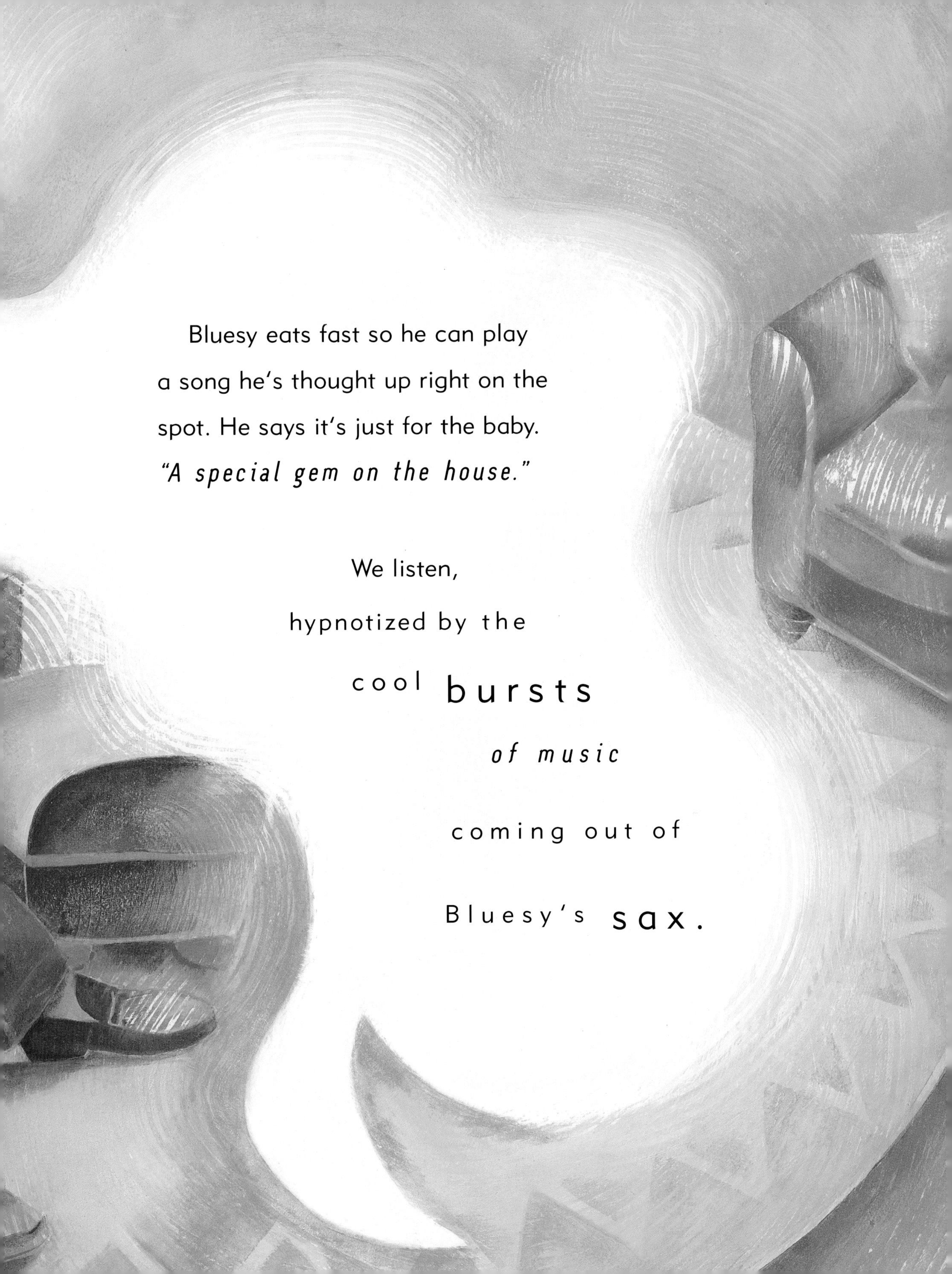

Bluesy eats fast so he can play a song he's thought up right on the spot. He says it's just for the baby. *"A special gem on the house."*

We listen,

hypnotized by the

cool **bursts**

of music

coming out of

Bluesy's **sax.**

Suddenly Ma knocks over the syrup and it drips to the floor.

"The baby's comin'!"

she cries, holding her belly.

We drive to the hospital in Bluesy's van.

Ma leans on Daddy as she sways on down the hall.

Bluesy and I wait in a white room,
waiting for Ma to have her baby.

Bluesy plays his
special gems
for the baby,
as softly as he can.
It's a long, *long*
time to wait.

At last, Daddy rushes toward us.

"It's a girl!" he says.

Bluesy and I run in to see Ma.

She looks tired and happy, her face glowing. She's holding a baby in her arms. "Come see your sister," Ma says, smiling big.

I come to the side of the bed and look closely at the baby. She has tufts of hair and dark, mad eyes.

She starts **wailing.**

"Hey, she looks kind of like me!" I say.

"Let's call her Gem," Ma says. "Thanks to Bluesy, Gem's her name and she's even got her own song."

Bluesy blushes and

starts in on

Gem's *gem.*

"On the house *special,*" he says.

Soon, Gem stops wailing.

We wonder at our new baby

and listen to

Bluesy's music

slipping around us

like a

cool sheet—

like moonlight,

and a

spring breeze.